Cool Classics
Level Two

For Piano Solo
Compiled and Arranged by Wesley Schaum

Forword

This book offers a unique approach to classics for the piano student. Familiar themes by classic composers are presented in two, and sometimes three sections forming a medley. In the first section, the theme is arranged in traditional style. The second and third sections are written in contrasting and embellished versions. Many of the embellishments are lighthearted caricatures with syncopations in a jazzy style. Others are enhanced with contemporary harmonies, imaginative bass lines and counter melodies.

Students will enjoy the stylistic changes and subtle humor that makes these pieces fun to play and terrific for recitals. This series consists of three books, Level 2, Level 3 and Level 4.

Index

Schaum Publications, Inc. • **10235 N. Port Washington Rd.** • **Mequon, WI 53092**
www.schaumpiano.net

In the Hall of the Mountain King

(from "Peer Gynt")

Edvard Grieg (1843-1907)

Meno mosso ♩ = 132-144 *(swing 8ths)*

Surprise Symphony

(Symphony No.94)

Franz Joseph Haydn (1732-1809)

Allegro ♩ = 132-144

Für Elise

Moderato ♩ = 108-120

Ludwig van Beethoven (1770-1827)

The Happy Farmer

(from "Album for the Young")

Giocoso ♩ = 152-168

Robert Schumann (1810-1856)

Allegro

(K3)

Allegro ♩ = 160-176

Wolfgang Amadeus Mozart (1756-1791)

Can Can

(from "La Vie Parisienne")

Jacques Offenbach (1819-1880)

Spring Song

(Op.62, No.6)

Cantabile ♩ = 144-160

Felix Mendelssohn (1809-1847)

Minuet in G Major

Allegretto ♩= 112-120

Johann Sebastian Bach (1685-1750)

Humoresque

(Op.101, No.7)

Anton Dvorak (1841-1904)

Allegretto ♩. = 80-92

21

Blue Danube Waltz

(Op.314)

Johann Strauss, Jr. (1825-1899)